BEHIND THE RHYMES

The random ramblings of an old duffer

Written and illustrated by John Trueman

Behind the Rhymes

Behind the Rhymes

For Luna (when she's a big girl)

Behind the Rhymes

BEHIND THE RHYMES

CONTENTS

Behind the Rhymes

Behind the Rhymes

BERT'S 'OLIDAY

To be read in a northern accent (apologies to anyone living north of Swindon)

Me and Bert's just back from Cyprus,
Ee – it were a lovely couple o' weeks.
Mind you, it would 'ave been much better,
With no Turkish and no Greeks.

Bert said 'e didn't like the plane,
And when I asked 'im why,
'e said the windows were too small,
You just see clouds and bits of sky.

The sun were 'ot, shined every day,
Bert's ears got burnt and red,
E's got a nose like Rudolph,
And e's peelin' on 'is 'ead.

When t'rep met us at t'hotel,
She said no bog paper down the pan.
She said that's one thing you can't do.
Bert said, I bloody can.

We didn't eat food in t'hotel,
It were oily – you could smell it.
And Bert said 'e'd not eat anything.
If 'e couldn't read or spell it.

Behind the Rhymes

So we found a lovely little caff.
Bert said that'll do for me.
They done fish and chips and beans on toast.
And baps wi' Typhoo tea.

Bert didn't like t'hotel lager,
But we found a pub quite near.
Where I 'ad port and lemon,
And Bert 'ad John Smith's beer.

Oh, and we found a nice McDonalds,
We ate there lots – 'twere easy,
Chips weren't as good as them at 'ome,
They were white and limp and greasy.

We didn't go to beach much.
Although it were all right,
Bert said the sand were far too 'ot.
And the sea, it smelt like shite.

We didn't like the pool much -
Full of kiddies 'avin' fun.
So we just sat on our balcony.
Smoking fags and and readin' t'Sun.

We got on well wi' t'other folk.
Except some posh bloke from down south.
'e said northerners were violent,
So Bert thumped 'im in the mouth.

Behind the Rhymes

We didn't understand the Euro,
Bert said, "Just makes things dear."
But ee, we 'ad a lovely time.
We're goin' back next year.

MEGHAN TOAST

To celebrate the engagement and marriage of Harry and Meghan

When Hairy aksed me to be his wife
I had to consider the rest of my life.
I wanted to know, will I wear a crown?
Will we live in a castle in old London town?

Will I have diamonds, pearls and gold rings?
Will I meet dooks and princes and kings?
Will I ride a gold carriage, pulled by white horses?
Will I inspect all of England's armed forces?

Will I get in free to Royal Ascot races?
Will servants wash my intimate places?
Will I have antiques and paintings and cars,
And cute liddle puppies and chocolate bars?

When we're in Scotchland, will I shoot game?
Will I have ocean liners to name?
Will we eat burgers from Royal Daulton poddery?
Of course. I'll mairy Hairy – it's like winning the loddery.

Behind the Rhymes

GOODBYE TO GOOD MATES

For Colin Venn and Baldy Goodenough, both from Pinehurst. Swindon

God was twiddling his thumbs up in Heaven,
Feeling quite bored with his lot,
So he called over Angel Gabriel,
And between them they hatched up a plot.

God decided they wanted new faces,
But only good blokes would do,
So he studied all people from Pinehurst,
And discovered the ideal two.

God gave his henchman an order,
Go snatch Venny, the first of the pair,
But be quick 'cos we don't want to lose him,
And the Devil wants him down there.

And while you're there, he instructed,
Saving young Colin from Hell,
We'll really piss off the Devil,
So bring Baldy Goodenough as well.

This turned out an inspired decision,
For Heaven, they were perfect blokes.
Venny helped God put the world right,
Whilst Baldy just kept telling jokes.

MADE ME VERY CROSS WORD

Crosswords are my relaxation,
But this one's causing much vexation.
I've scratched my head and chewed my pen,
Studied, scratched and chewed again.

It is U, space, U, space, U, space, space.
A word my brain just cannot place.
Seven letters, three of which are U,
As yet, I haven't got a clue.

Actually, I have – it's 7 down,
It's the answer causing me to frown.
The cryptic clue just reads, "Rare word,"
Which is blatantly obvious and absurd.

U, Space, U, space, U, space and space?
I'm scrolling through my mental database.
It's uncommon, extraordinary, scarce, sporadic,
Bizarre, abnormal or erratic,
Exceptional, atypical, unique, infrequent,
Occasional, exceptional, intermittent,
Matchless, singular, scarce or few,
With a steak it's bloody, juicy, blue.

U, space, U, space, U, space and space ?
Is the answer staring me in the face?
No! I've given up this mental duel,
Because this word is so unusual.

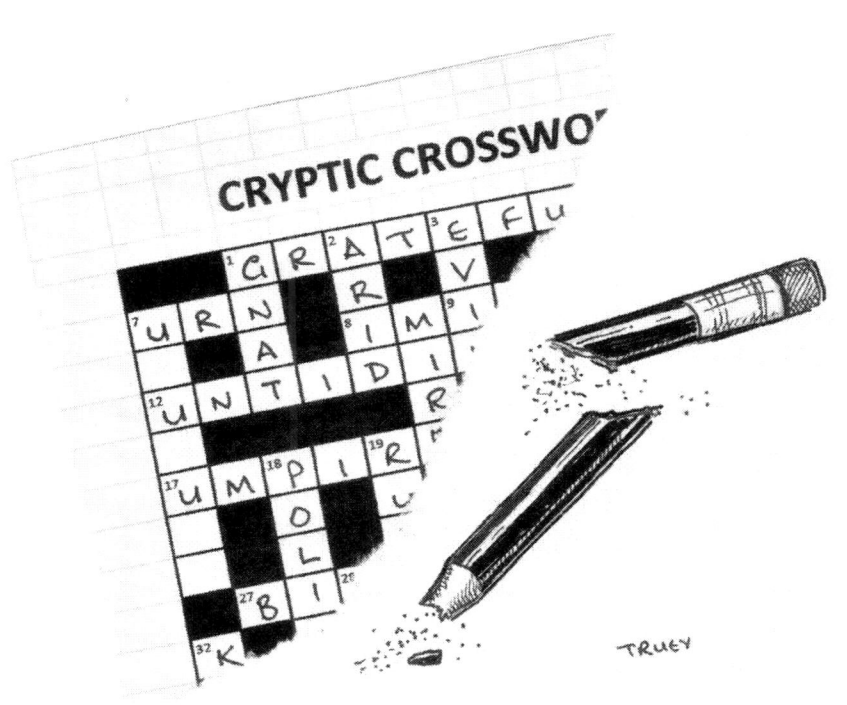

WILLIE'S OLD JOKES

For Mick Wiltshire – his favourite and oft-repeated jokes

I said to my mate Willie,
"Something odd happened today,
A strange lady smiled and waved at me,
And then went on her way.

She was in a big farm vehicle
Huge wheels, you know the one,"
Willie said, "A tractor?"
I said, "I must have done."

I said "I've just acquired a dog,
Looks like a small greyhound."
Willie thought, and then said "Whippet?"
I said, "No, I paid a pound."

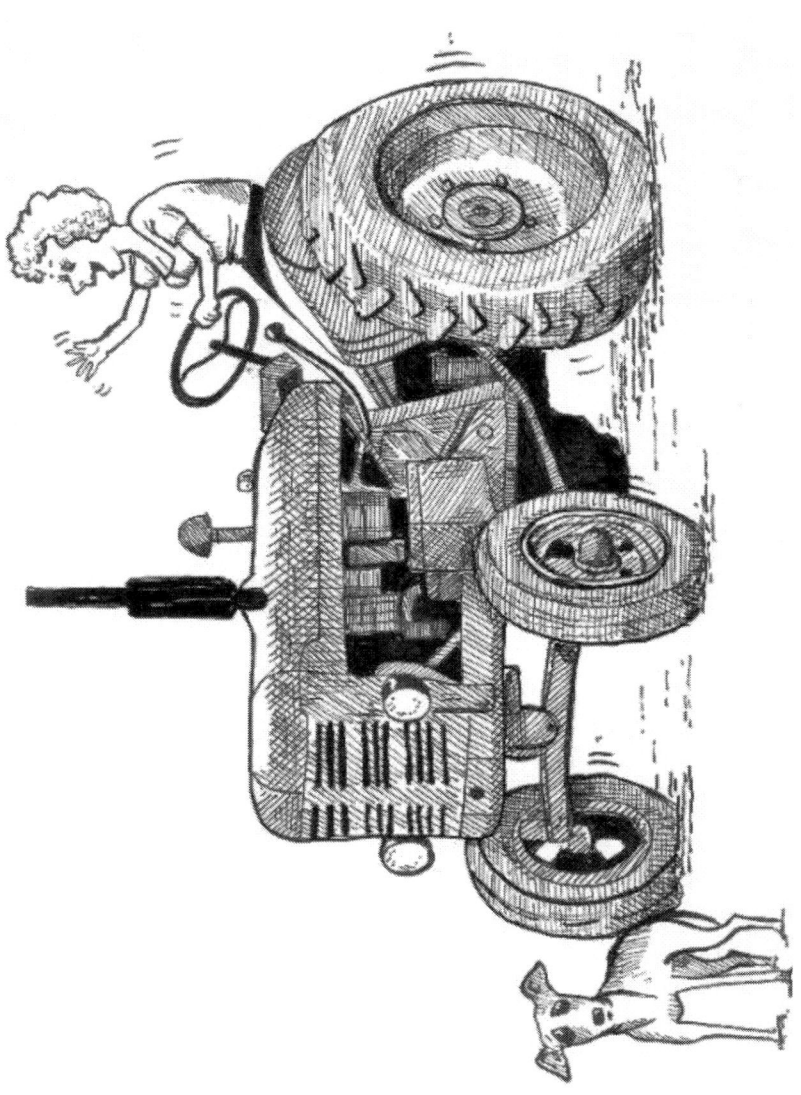

CONDIMENTS OF THE SEASON

Why salt is used on icy roads,

Has left me quite confused.

As pepper's hot and salt is not,

Why isn't pepper used?

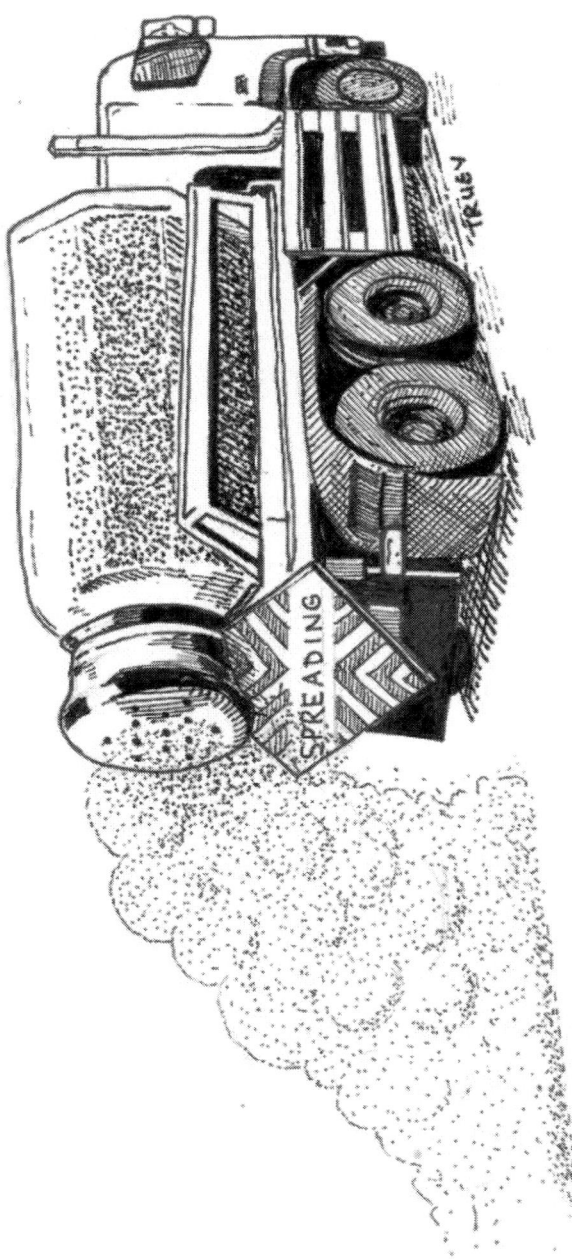

Behind the Rhymes

NO DOGS SPOTTED

I've been to the Dalmation coast,

To the country of Croatia,

The thing there that surprised me most,

Dogs aren't spotty in Dalmatia.

Behind the Rhymes

MEN OF GOD

With apologies to no-one

Whilst I hold nothing against religion,
I have my doubts - more than a smidgen.
I hope that this is not profanity,
But I distrust people of Christianity.

Bishops have the most authority,
But to me are cloaked in inferiority.
To say a parson is parsimonious,
I do not think would be erroneous.

Whilst preachers are known to preachify,
Do rectors always rectify?
And are most reverends reverential?
In my experience it's not essential.

Vicars think themselves vicarious,
But I find them to be contrarious.
Pastoral may define a pastor,
But most, I feel, are a disaster.

Priests I do not find prestigious,
Their acts are often irreligious.
Clerics think themselves quite clerical,
Whilst I find most of them hysterical.

Behind the Rhymes

Monks to me seem far too serious,
And I've never seen a nun delirious.
Are ministers always ministerial?
To me they always seem ethereal.

They all claim to be good and just,
But there's not one bugger that I'd trust.

MY DRIVING

I don't drive so much now, as a septuagenarian,
But I do find other drivers most humanitarian.
When I pop to the shop or attend a meeting,
Strangers shout and wave to offer a greeting.

As I potter to town, cars drive close behind me,
Flashing their headlights, I guess to remind me,
How well I am driving, so I respond with smiles,
As they continue to follow and flash me for miles.

When I am parking, others look overawed,
They point and laugh and then they applaud.
When roundabouts baffle me and I suddenly brake,
Drivers hold up two fingers, for the exit to take.

On roads in the country, men honk as we pass.
And, for a joke, they'll drive up on the grass.
Then they just sit with a feigned look of fright,
Before waving their fists to show they're alright.

Accidents? Me? No. I've not had any:
Although, I must say, I tend to see many.

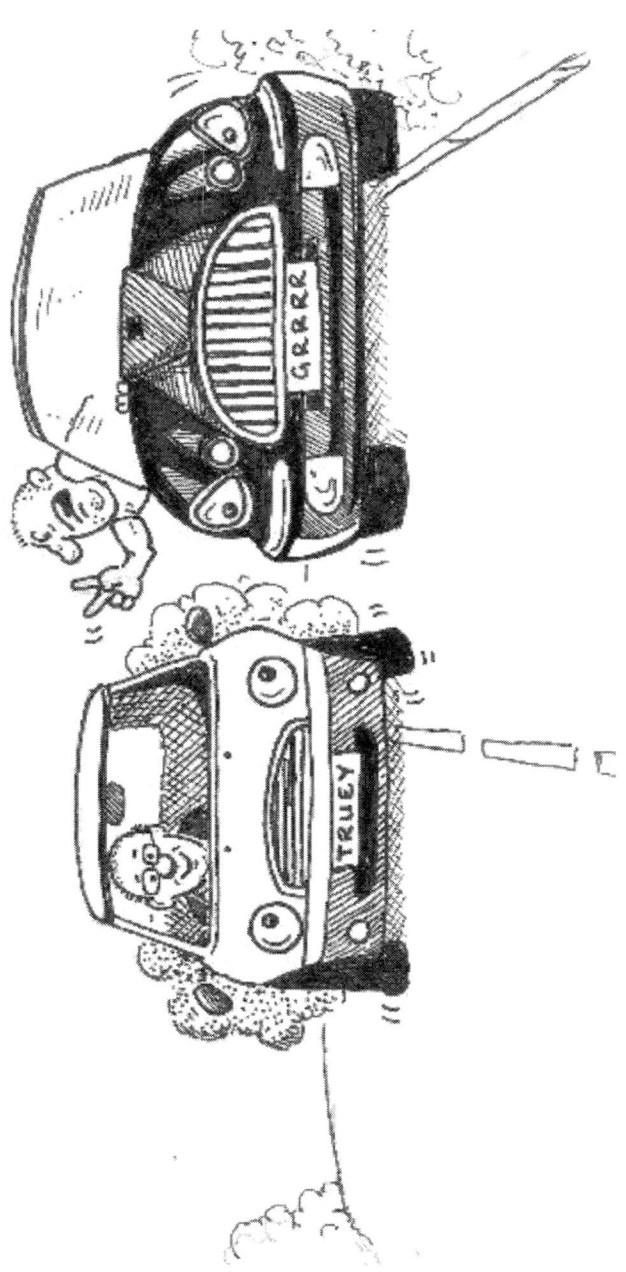

Behind the Rhymes

THERE WAS A YOUNG POET

A young poet right in his prime,
Wrote limericks, sharp and sublime,
But then his heart sank,
And his mind went quite blank,
As he couldn't find words that would correspond the
sound between words or the endings of words, especially
when used at the ends of lines of poetry.

With apologies to Edward Lear

THE WIFE AND ME

For Sue on our forty-first anniversary

My wife likes her eggs hard-boiled,
I like my boiled eggs soft and runny.
I like the weather fresh and cool,
She likes it warm and sunny.

She likes pasta and salad with sauces,
Ribbon vegetables with exotic dips,
I prefer meat pies and sausage,
With baked beans and piles of chips.

She loves it when we go shopping,
A pastime that I find a chore,
I prefer to go and watch football,
Something that she finds a bore.

She dresses in smart stylish fashion,
Always elegant, looking her best.
I wear old joggers and slippers,
With dinner dribbled on my vest.

She only drinks fine filter coffee,
Whilst I slurp tea made with a bag.
Sometimes she'll sip a small *rosé,*
I swig beer from the can, with a fag.

Behind the Rhymes

She likes TV documentaries,
History and nature and news.
I like sport and old comedies.
Or to sit there and have a nice snooze.

There seems no way we are well-suited,
Except being father and mother,
The only thing that we agree on…
…Is that we love each other.

Apologies to Fredrick Richardson

ONE PENCE

Because it really annoys me

No-one says, "One pounds," nor do they say, "One dollars,"
One never says, "One Euros" or "One cents."
So why do many people, even educated scholars,
Erroneously use the term "*One pence*.?"

ROSES ARE PINK

On Valentine's Day, the cards all say,

That roses are red and violets are blue,

Yet, the colour "rose" is really pink,

And violets have a violet hue.

TOLERANCE

As I am now well into my eighth decade,
I have become liberal, and am no longer swayed,
By unfounded prejudices. I am not blinded
By preconceptions. I am open-minded.

I now understand we are not all the same.
No longer will I judge or condemn or blame,
It is important that differences can be embraced,
Although awkward, diversity must be freely faced.

That said, I find some men uncouth,
Especially those who cling to youth,
By dying their hair or wearing an earring,
Inanely adorned with phoney veneering.

People who play loud music from cars,
And men wearing vests in the street or in bars,
And older women festooned with tattoos,
Those wobbling around in ridiculous shoes.

Those who eat or drink whilst walking along,
Men who pose on the beach, wearing a thong,
And those who drop litter, mainly fast-food containers,
And, of course, all Brexit remainers.

Behind the Rhymes

Fat but mobile folk on mobility scooters,
Those permanently attached to phones or computers.
Laddish young ladies who think they are daring,
By drinking lager and casually swearing.

Teenagers slouching in their hooded tops,
Assistants who ignore me when I'm in shops
Overpaid but inept presenters on air,
So-called comedians who do nothing but swear,

I hate cooking experts and talent shows,
And men wearing perfume get right up my nose.
All reality tele, I really despise,
And all politicians, telling nothing but lies.

And old people's mumbling and young people's yammer,
And text speak, poor English and incorrect grammar,
And the inability to use correct punctuation,
Are the ruination of this once great nation.

I can't stand cyclists who get in my way,
Officious officials and children at play,
Those allowing dogs to soil public spaces,
And graffiti vandals who deface public places.

I don't much care for those under fifty,
Men wearing beards, to me, look too shifty.
Pretentious wine experts pontificating,
And all modern art I find infuriating.

Behind the Rhymes

Whilst my heart's full of love for my fellow man.
There is one group of people I wish I could ban,
Though I regard most as my sisters and brothers,
I'd exterminate those intolerant of others.

A COWBOY'S LAMENT

Simply to amuse Ricky Bowling, my fellow cowboy fan

I should have been a cowboy,
Like Audie Murphy or John Wayne,
Driving herds of cattle,
Across the great American plain.

I could have been a cowboy,
In the saddle for miles and miles,
And I **would** have been a cowboy,
If it wasn't for my piles.

I'd ride the Chisholm Trail,
From Texas down to Abilene,
From San Antonio and El Paso,
With longhorns, lean and mean.

We'd cross the big Red River,
And break mustangs at Fort Worth,
I was meant to be a cowboy,
That's why I'm on this Earth.

I'd be pals with Randolph Scott,
James Stewart and Tom Mix,
Gary Cooper and John Wayne would come,
Whenever we were in a fix.

Behind the Rhymes

I'd play guitar with Gene Autrey,
I'd play poker with Buck Jones,
I'd drink Red Eye with Tex Ritter,
To take the chill out of my bones,

"Rope 'em, tie 'em, brand 'em,"
That's the job that I espouse.
And I know I could have done it,
If I wasn't scared of cows.

I'd ride my palomino stallion,
Through the days and nights,
Except that horses are quite big,
And I'm afraid of heights.

In the evening I'd kick off my boots,
And just dust down my jeans,
I'd sit around the campfire,
Singing songs and eating beans,

But the other cowboys probably,
Would make me sit apart,
Because my voice is squeaky,
And beans always make me fart.

We would have to fight off Indians,
To save our precious prize,
As they fire their flaming arrows,
With the whoops of their war cries,

Behind the Rhymes

We'd fire back with our Winchesters,
Or Colt 45's perhaps,
But I wouldn't want to hurt them.
They seem quite decent chaps.

I may even be a rustler,
That really wouldn't worry me.
Except that my wife says that,
I couldn't rustle up a cup of tea.

Or I might have been a sheriff,
Out to catch the outlaw gangs,
With shootouts in Dodge City,
Except I don't like loud "bangs."

I could have been a cowboy,
I could, I really could.
Except, on reflection,
I may not have been much good.

It's true to say I must accept
That I would not be the best,
So I'll just stay in Somerset,
In England's Wild West.

Behind the Rhymes

With apologies to Thelwell

TECHNO-ZOMBIES

Eyes down, the techno-zombie,
Walks blindly on the street,
Shoulders hunched and head dropped,
On shuffling, stumbling feet.

Not seeing where she's going,
Not knowing where she's been,
Eyes fixed and unblinking,
Spellbound by her electronic screen.

Techno-zombie lovers meet,
for their first romantic date.
The sweethearts staring at their phones.
Romance, it seems, can wait.

Even Orwell could not prophesy,
The control of their Big Brother,
Communicating with the world,
Whilst ignoring one another.

The child plays in the rockpool,
Discovering natures miracles.
Studying crabs and shrimps, gills and shells,
And wondrous spiracles.

He looks to share his treasures,
But, sadly, plays alone,
While Techno-zombie parents,
Are reading drivel on their phone.

Behind the Rhymes

The family walks the countryside,
Trees alive with singing birds,
The teenagers hear nothing,
As Techno-zombie nerds.

Ignoring chaffinch chatter,
Robin's song and caw of crow.
Preferring electronic tweets,
From twits they barely know.

Facebook, Twitter, Youtube, Instagram and Snapchat -
E-mails, Messenger, notifications and photos of a cat.
Messages from Whatsapp, half-truths from Wikipedia -
All of them brain-numbing, antisocial bloody media!

ENOUGH!

Of all the vagaries in English speech,
There's one that always makes me wonder.
Why rough and tough are rhymed with muff,
Is this just a pronuncial blunder?

Trough is troff and chough is chuff,
It makes me think enough's enuff.
More oddly, hiccough rhymes with sup,
Yet cough is not pronounced as cup.

Though Slough will always rhyme with cow,
Through rhymes with shoe and bough with bow,
But bow itself can rhyme with hoe,
As indeed can though and dough.

And even when you swap a letter,
Laugh is laff, which is no better.
This elocution still seems daft,
As draught will always rhyme with raft.

Then bought and fought will rhyme with taut,
And, you'll agree, will sought and caught.
And ought and wrought and nought and fraught.
And so, quite naturally, will taught.

The clue to this mixed enunciation,
Is summed by the articulation:
Of the end of words thorough and borough
Where the final syllable is **UGH!**

A RIGHT ROYAL KNEES-UP?

I wonder what the Queen does at Christmas.
I wonder what she does on Christmas day.
I expect she has to get up really early,
To start cooking while the family's on their way.

She probably has to make her Philip's breakfast,
A bacon sarnie or fried egg on toast,
Before she starts to get the Christmas dinner,
Which is probably a turkey roast.

First, she'll have to get the veggies ready,
Preparing sprouts and parsnips, and the spuds.
I bet she uses frozen ones from Waitrose,
Along with Auntie Bessie's Yorkshire puds.

And then she'll make some real Paxo stuffing,
Which the royals always nibble with their meat.
She'll open up a pack of Bisto gravy,
And that red jam that only posh folk eat.

I don't know if she'll have a real a turkey,
Roasted to a lovely golden brown.
I'd like to think that, due to her position,
She prefers to cook a Norfolk turkey crown.

Behind the Rhymes

And when the family comes, they'll all swop presents,
Whilst munching on their chocolates, nuts and fruit,
The queen will get some scent and perfumed soap,
And the princes get cigars and packs of Brut.

Then while Queen and the princesses lay the table,
The princes will get ready for the pub,
Just a couple of quick ones dear, they will promise,
And vow to be home by two, in time for grub.

When the men come back, everyone get dressed up,
The Queen puts on her crown and a long frock,
All the princes will wear their best sailor suits,
Except for Charles, in his kilt, just like a Jock.

After they have finished all their dinner,
And had enough of pudding and of booze.
The queen will start to clear away the dishes,
While the men will have a well-earned little snooze.

When the Queen has finished clearing up the dinner,
She'll probably watch herself on the TV,
Then she'll have to start to lay the table,
With cold meats, cakes and jelly for their tea.

And when Christmas day is nearly over,
And the last of the chores are finally done,
All the family have gone home to their own houses,
She'll tell Phil, "That really was not fun.

Behind the Rhymes

Next year one will do something quite different,
Where one will not be treated like a common char.
One will go and visit one's historic relations,
Frohe Weihnachten und ein glückliches Neues Jahr!" *

*Merry Christmas and Happy New Year

THE PUB

In Requiem

Whatever's 'appened to the country pub?
Whatever's 'appened to our locals?
They were once a refuge for the drinking man,
Full of jolly, happy, drinking yokels.

Whatever's 'appened to the ambiance,
The welcome smell of fags and beers,
Plain walls yellowed by the nicotine,
Wood floors mellowed by the years.

Whatever's 'appened to the ale 'ouse,
Once a place of ribald cheer?
They're wine bars, gastros, bistros now,
Selling anything but beer.

Whatever's 'appened to our proper drinks,
Mild and bitter, brown or light?
With Babycham for ladies,
Port and lemon, Saturday night.

Young 'uns now drink foreign lager,
Or liqueurs and alcopops,
And poncy wines like Prosecco,
Or, God 'elp us, shots.

Behind the Rhymes

Whatever's 'appened to the barmaid,
All smiles and bouncing chest?
So when she bent to pull a pint,
You could glimpse a bit of breast.

Whatever's 'appened to the landlord,
Red-faced, pot-bellied and funny?
Now there's just a faceless manager,
In 'is office, counting money.

What's 'appened to the click of dominoes,
Or the thud, thud, thud of darts?
Now there's just a giant bloody screen,
Blasting pop videos from the charts.

Whatever's 'appened to the characters,
Telling far-fetched tales and jokes?
Now they're huddled in the street,
To enjoy their harmless smokes.

Whatever's 'appened to the toilets,
In a corrugated shed across the yard?
Now it's mood music and urinals,
And decorated "*avant-garde.*"

What's 'appened to the cheap night out?
Tippin' eight pints down your throat.
A bag of chips on the way home,
Change from a ten pound note.

Behind the Rhymes

The pub trade's burning just like Rome,
And, like Nero, owners fiddle,
And blokes like me are staying 'ome,
Drinkin' beer and wine from Lidl.

AITCH

Of twenty-six letters in our alphabet,
One is solitary, lonely, absurd,
It's the only one that can be spelt,
AITCH is the lone five-letter word.

A is not written on paper as AYE.
And B is not printed as BEE,
Whilst F can't be written as EFF,
And C's not recorded as SEA.

I is not EYE and L never ELL,
And there is no EMM, EN or JAY,
R is not ARE and S is not ESS,
And no-one would write K as KAY.

X is not EXE, and Y is not WHY?
And Q is never spelt CUE,
No-one I know, would write V as VEE,
And W's not DOUBLE-YOU.

U is not YOU and we don't spell Z ZED,
Even Americans don't spell Z ZEE,
Of the letters we've left, DEE doesn't spell D
And there is no EE, GEE, PEA or TEA.

Behind the Rhymes

Yet AITCH is a one-off exception,
As a word that is commonly used,
Not only that, but AITCH is unique,
In the way that it's oft abused.

When starting a word, AITCH is often ignored,
Honour and Honest make AITCH superfluous,
In other words, too, it is often snubbed,
As in ghost or aghast or Rhinosaurus.

Though it is often pronounced incorrectly,
It's strange AITCH does not start with H,
I once heard a man say, "'ere 'Arry,
Does 'Arrow on the 'Ill 'ave a HAITCH?"

THE COCKLE PICKER

Written during a previous life in Portugal

I saw a cockle picker,
Picking cockles yesterday.
I said, "I'd like to try my hand,
At cockle picking, if I may."

"If you want to pick some cockles,"
The cockle picker said,
"Come and pick some cockles,
In my cockle picking bed."

I started picking cockles,
And soon had the technique licked.
Then went to show the cockle picker,
All the cockles that I'd picked.

The cockle picker studied,
All the cockles in my sack,
And said, "The cockles that you've picked,
Will have to be put back.

When it comes to cockle pickers lad,
I've never met one thicker,
You've got your molluscs muddled up
You're just a winkle picker."

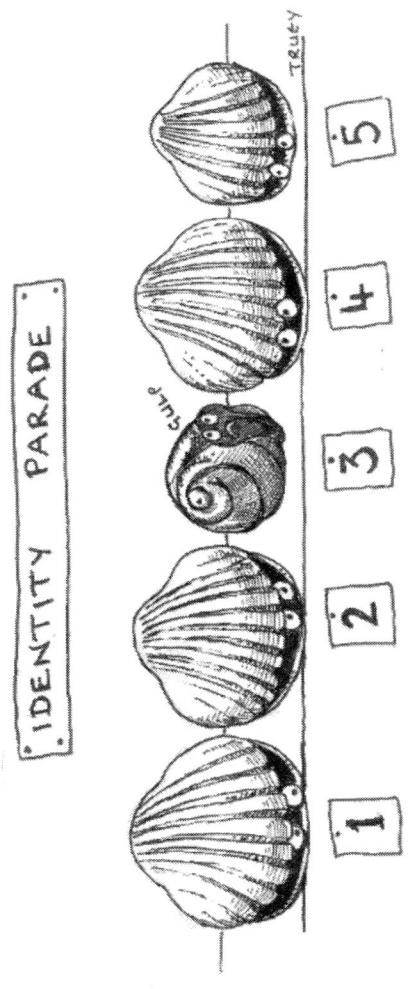

DOING MY BIT

For Teddy and Jack Trueman

Grandpy was soldier of the trenches,
In muddy Hell, amongst the dead.
He sought no praise and no reward,
"Just doin' me bit," he said.

My father followed his footsteps.
A desert rat of World War Two.
At Dunkirk, Tobruk, El Alemein
He just did his bit too.

My generation are the lucky ones
With no worldwide altercations,
Yet, beneath this sense of gratitude,
I admit to deep frustrations.

For reasons that I can't explain.
There's a huge void in my life,
Unable just test myself,
In times of war and strife.

I feel my life is incomplete,
As a proud and patriotic Brit.
I wonder, would I be brave enough,
If called upon to do my bit?

Behind the Rhymes

Would I have been the first in line,
To answer's Britain's call?
To be prepared to give my life,
 When backed against the wall.

I'll never know the comradeship,
As the lads did in the past,
Of fighting evil with my mates,
Knowing this day may be our last

Yet Remembrance Day, frustration shelved,
My poppy's worn with pride,
Lest we forget those, who did their bit,
Those who fought and died.

DUBROVNIC

My wife and I love lakes and mountains,
Ignoring palaces, churches, fountains,
We've never understood the cities' lure,
Preferring forests, hills and moor.

Though pastoral peace is really "us,"
Impulsively, we took a bus,
To visit ancient Dubrovnic,
Despite our qualms of stone and brick.

In the old town, we saw the appeal,
The sense of history was very real,
Impressive walls and gates and towers,
Historic houses, festooned by flowers.

The enchantment to us, as rural purists,
Was soon overwhelmed by gangs of tourists,
Disgorged from taxis, buses and coaches,
Scurrying about like plagues of roaches.

Passengers herded from their cruise ships,
Holidaymakers on their day trips,
Trudging the streets, tired and baggy-eyed,
Bored by constant spiel from their guide.

Packs of Americans in ragged formation,
Loud shirts and loud voices from a loud nation,
Blindly following their scheduled tour,
Finding Europe a tiresome bore.

Behind the Rhymes

"Shall we see the monastery dear?"
"No, you go honey, I'll wait for you here."
"Let's dodge the museum. There's one at home,
Besides, we saw one last week in Rome."

Chinese and Japanese, clogging up places,
Taking photographs of their faces.
First ensuring they're looking their best,
Selfie-indulgent, selfie-obsessed.

Gangs of Russians, stone-faced and ashen,
An invading army in eighties fashion.
Competing with Germans, glaring while waiting,
To see who could look the most intimidating.

Sponza Place, Pile Gate, Stradum and more,
Smothered by trippers, tired and footsore,
Restaurants selling burgers and chips,
Noisy boat-owners touting their trips.

Fat-bellied Brits full of holiday cheer,
Looking for bars that sell English beer.
Scouring the shops for cheap tourist tat,
Dressed in a vest and kiss-me-quick hat.

The historic splendour soon dissipated,
Our high expectations quickly deflated.
Misted by hustle and bustle and noise,
More tacky and tawdry than style and poise.

Behind the Rhymes

Can those who profit from selling the dream,
Not see soured milk curdling under the cream?
One day the cash cow will surely run dry,
It's not *do kasnije* Dubrovnik, but goodbye.

Behind the Rhymes

ANIMAL AGM

At their AGM the animals met,
In a spirit of collusion,
And there agreed the first thing to debate.
They discussed how varied languages,
Were causing great confusion,
They would choose a common tongue,
Before it was too late.

The Howler monkey howled,
That the language should be Howl,
With Shriek or Hoot suggested,
By an aggravated owl.

The dog was most dogmatic,
That the language should be Bark.
Tweet was then proposed,
By a quite indignant lark.

The cat thought it catastrophic,
To have anything but Mew.
Whilst a wildebeest from Africa,
Was convinced they should talk Gnu.

The donkey was most stubborn
In putting forward Bray,
His cousin, horse, was hoarse,
In insisting it was Neigh.

Behind the Rhymes

Sheep were very sheepish,
When they put forward Baa.
The crows were crowing loudly,
That a better choice was Kaa,

Bull was bullish stating,
That the language should be Moo
And the cow would not be cowed,
Because she wanted Moo too.

The elephant was elegant,
In recommending Trump,
And the camel spat that all this talk,
Was giving him the hump.

The boar was bored but still proposed,
The language should be Snort,
The Warthog then agreed with him,
After first submitting Wart.

The lion and the tiger,
Jointly put forward Roar,
And glared around ominously,
Seeking support from the floor.

The wallaby was wobbly,
And the duck just ducked the issue,
The deer just said, "Dear dear,"
And cried into a tissue.

Behind the Rhymes

The ewe then made a bleating sound,
By blowing her euphonium.
The panda pandered to the ewe,
Which created pandemonium.

The frog and toad said jointly,
That the language should be Croak,
The hyena started laughing,
Because he thought it was joke.

Eagles were egalitarian,
The kangaroo was rude,
The baboon showed his bottom,
And then said something lewd.

The giraffe stuck his neck out,
But had nothing much to say,
The rabbit kept on rabbiting,
That it was too late in the day.

The parrot parroted other birds,
The leopard changed its spots.
The meeting collapsed in chaos,
No-one knowing who said what.

Finally the animals agreed
That there could not be a winner,
The lion stared at the antelope,
And growled, "Let's break for dinner."

Behind the Rhymes

REMEMBER WHEN…?

To celebrate an old Alanbrooke Football Club mate's 70th birthday (which turned out to be his 69th)

Two old boys sat in the pub,
Quietly reminiscing,
Of music, cars and girls,
Things in old age they were missing.

But they mostly talked of football,
And playing for Alanbrooke,
The passes, tackles, goals,
And the penalties they took.

The two men laughed as they recalled,
The fun that they had had.
They laughed about the good times
And smiled about the bad.

Then in tranquil contemplation,
They sat in private thought,
Of battles won and battles lost,
And battles bravely fought.

They thought of pals and team-mates,
And enemies they'd crossed,
Of where their many friends were now,
And of friends that they had lost.

Behind the Rhymes

One man's name escaped them,
That of a young defender.
They thought he came from Moredon.
He was strong and tall and slender.

Good with ball, great in the air,
They used all their recall powers,
And when he played with Wirdnam,
They were known as the Twin Towers.

They thought that he was Bill or Bert,
And Holly, Colly, Colic?
"No, no, cried one, I've got it now.
We're thinking of Ben Hollick."

The other chap grinned widely,
And punched the air in glee,
"Ben Hollick, I remember now.
Ben Hollick – that is me!"

WILLIE LOTT'S COTTAGE

A shabby cottage by the Stour,
Was owned by Willie Lott,
His wife told Willie, "Decorate -
Or live there, I will not!"

She nagged poor Willie night and day,
Complaint after complaint,
That it sorely needed sprucing up,
Starting with a lick of paint.

"I'd do it dear," said Willie Lott,
"But I can't paint, that's the rub,"
"Then find a painter," said his wife,
"There'll be one down the pub."

"Do you know a painter, landlord?"
Willie asked when in The Swan.
The landlord said, "Try that bloke there,"
He's a painter, name of John.

John agreed to paint the house,
While Willie was away.
He said, "It's only twenty quid,
Have a good holiday."

Behind the Rhymes

When Willie and his wife got home,
They both felt quite bereft.
It seemed to them their cottage,
Was the same as when they left.

Willie rushed off to The Swan,
And confronted painter John.
He asked why the painting wasn't done,
While he and wife were gone.

"Not paint your cottage?" John exclaimed,
"I definitely did.
Look, I've got the painting here,
Now where's my twenty quid?"

And John produced a picture,
Neatly painted, nicely framed.
"You can see that it's your house,
And you should be ashamed!"

The picture was of Willie's house,
Of that there was no doubt,
But it wasn't what he wanted,
So he began to shout,

"That's not what I asked for,
And I'm not going to pay.
Besides the picture's spoilt,
There's a hay wain in the way.

Behind the Rhymes

That picture's not worth twenty quid,
And you're solely responsible,
So you know what you can do.
Keep your painting, Mr Constable!"

TRUEY

CRIMEAN WAR

The cause of the Crimean War seems quite nebulous,
Though the conflict was fought with honour and passion,
Yet, its best-known legacy is almost incredulous,
That is, the naming of items of gentlemen's fashion.

Sevastopol and Gallipoli have passed into history,
Little more than exotic names on a map,
Yet the Battle of Balaclava's no mystery,
Because it gave its name to a warm, woolly cap.

The Duke of Wellington was a leader and statesman,
Although twice prime minister, few give a hoot.
In history, what is best known of this great man,
Is that he gave name to a black, knee-length boot.

Lord Cardigan, though a soldier, has passed into lore,
For his button-up woollie, we are led to believe.
Lord Raglan who bravely fought and died in this war,
Is mainly remembered because of his sleeve.

This naming phenomena has long made me wonder:
When the Light Brigade charged their ill-fated advance,
Were other clothes named from this military blunder?
Sergeant Brown-Trousers or Private Stained-UnderPants?

HENRI TOULOUSE-LAUTREC

Written in Franglais

Toulouse-Lautrec was an artiste célèbre,
A résidé à Paris, France,
Il aime relaxer at le Moulin Rouge,
A regarder des naked dames dance.

Une nuit, as he regardé the troupe,
Il pensait que son soul would combust,
Comme il a studied un nouveau danseur,
A été consumed avec un strong lust.

During la pause du spectacle,
Il followed le danseur backstage,
On en voyant her there, dans su tutu,
His passion ne could pas assuage.

Il boldly approché le jeune danseur,
And told her son heart would explode,
And they must make l'amour ensemble,
Immédiatement, ou son world would implode.

She said, "Ce n'est pas possible,"
Comme elle slipped on ses nouvelles ballet shoes.
"Nous ne make pas l'amour maintenant,
Parce que, il y a no time, Toulouse."

With apologies to M. Toulouse-Lautrec

SYRUP OF FIG

Nowadays a young chap losing hair,
Tends to shave his head,
The older man whose head is bare,
Has a comb-over instead.

Another may disguise his pate,
With a conspicuous wig.
Which proudly sits atop his dome,
Like a well-trained guinea pig.

It makes one ask, "What is the point,
When the world knows it's sham?"
Though people mock the fellow,
Seems he does not give a damn.

Is he not worried, asinine,
In his narcissistic fug?
Or does he think that no-one knows…
…A smug mug in a rug?

Behind the Rhymes

ON THE WAGON?

Because I say this most days

I'm definitely giving up drinking.
I'm going to pack up the booze.
For a while now I have been thinking,
Abstinence is the right path to choose.

It's not that I *need* to drink beer.
I am certainly not alcoholic.
I do it to keep my head clear,
And to stave off colds, flu and colic.

I'm not hooked. I don't crave to sup.
It's certainly not an addiction.
I know that I *can* give it up.
I know I have the conviction.

I'm sure that it's better to quit.
I can do without a few beers.
Besides, my trousers don't fit.
And I've not seen my willy for years.

I pour my first pint each evening at six,
As soon as I hear the clock chime.
It's just a bad habit, but one I can fix.
I feel I should do more with my time.

Behind the Rhymes

Just think of the time I will gain,
And things I can do when I'm slim.
To improve both my body and brain,
Perhaps I'll join up at a gym.

I'll start yoga or reading good books.
I might take up poetry or art,
Or model my handsome new looks.
This really will be a new start.

My commitment's as firm as a rock.
I'll have no regrets and no sorrow.
Oh dear, it's now beer o'clock,
But I'm on the wagon…tomorrow.

SIZE MATTERS

There's a theory you may treat with caution,

Though most experts hold that it's true,

A penis has inverse proportion,

To the size of its owner's IQ.

ANGLLESEY

Sue and I have just returned.
From Anglesey, North Wales,
With stunning beaches, towering mountains,
Awe inspiring vales.

But navigation of this lovely isle,
Was cause for consternation,
The problem is the Welsh speak Welsh,
And use Welsh pronunciation.

Whenever we tried to find our way,
We ended up in trouble…well,
Wouldn't you when every place,
Begins with double L.

The exotic and mellifluous tongue,
I don't mean to belittle,
But when people told me where they lived,
I was covered in their spittle.

There's Llanbadrig, Llanddona and Llanbabo
Llanerchymedd, Llanfachraeth and Llanallgo.
Llanfaes, Llanfaethlu, Llantrisant,
Llanfugail, Llanfairyneubwll and Llanddeusant

And there's Llanfaelog and Llandyfrydog
Llanfairynghornwy, Llanfwrog, Llangwyllog
Llaingoch, Llangefni, Llangoed, Llangadwaladr,
Llangaffo Llangristiolus, Llanrhyddladand Llanddaniel,
Llansadwrn, Llanynghenedl, Llaneilian,
LlandegfanLlanfihangel, Yn Nhywyn and Llanfechell.

Behind the Rhymes

I am in awe of the Welsh tongue and do not mean to mock,
But couldn't they think of an easier name than...
Llanfairpwllgwyngyllgogerychwyrndrobwyllllantysiliogo
gogoch.

BRAIN SURGEON

Written to try to cheer up my oldest mate(unsuccessfully)

Brian Arbin was a surgeon,
Whose speciality was the brain,
He lived in Braintree Essex,
At number 1 Barn Lane.

His wife was called Sabrina,
And Barnie was their son.
His daughter was Robina,
Brianna was the youngest one.

The Arbins planned to go abroad,
To Albania or Bahrain,
Or perhaps to Bari or Nairobi,
They also looked at Spain.

Just to book the foreign holiday,
There were many forms to fill,
Insurance, passports, flights and visas,
The worry made poor Brian ill.

In the end they stayed in Britain…
Foreign planning was too hectic.
For Brian Arbin, brain surgeon,
Was diagnosed dyslexic.

"Oh, O..B..C..L..S..L..K..O……"

FAREWELL ALEC

In memory of my "Uncle-in-Law" and mate, Alec New

It's a sad farewell to Alec,
Good company, good mate, good bloke.
Each year, we'd meet and sink a few;
We'd drink and laugh and joke.

We both enjoyed a little drink,
– Not too much, but just sufficient,
We spent time playing a special game,
At which we became proficient.

When our ladies' backs were turned,
We gave a silent cheer,
And sneaked into the nearest bar,
For red wine and a beer.

When we went out for a meal we'd say,
"Stay there, we'll get the food."
Then to the bar for a quick one,
Just to get us in the mood.

On market days, we'd tell the girls,
"Go shopping, we'll be fine,"
Then pop into the nearest bar,
For a beer and red wine.

Behind the Rhymes

Nights in watching tele,
We'd wait for the girls to snooze,
Then nip down to the bar again,
For a little bit more booze.

Sunday mornings into town,
To pick up the English papers.
A brandy with our coffee,
Was the start of that day's capers.

Lunchtime off to Miguel's bar,
When we thought the girls weren't looking,
"Well," we said, "they don't want us,
- They're happy with the cooking."

We'd converse about a lot of things,
As only two chaps can,
Of cricket, football, wives and wine,
Chatting, man to man.

We'd talk of people that we'd known,
And things we did as lads.
The strain of being perfect,
Flawless husbands, faultless dads.

Sometimes we talked of life and death,
What happens when we die,
We both agreed we'd like to go,
To the big bar in the sky.

Behind the Rhymes

We laughed and said we'd meet again,
When we end our Earthly lives,
And the first one gets the round in,
For when the other one arrives.

Mine's a pint Alec.

MY SONNET

I've often wondered what a sonnet is,
So I studied those by Shakespeare the Bard,
With the sole aim of writing one like his,
But I admit I found the technique hard.
I understand that poems in this form,
Have fourteen lines if composed correctly,
Within each line, ten syllables are norm,
And every other line rhymes perfectly.
So now I understand what is needed,
My head is clear and my hand is steady,
Instructions have been carefully heeded,
I have my sheet of lined foolscap ready,
On which to pen a magnificent sonnet,
But I just can't think what to write on it.

FARMER AVERY

Farmer Avery was getting bored,
And found his farmwork rather bland,
So, he thought how to diversify,
And how he could expand.

The key was in his buildings,
So he converted barns to shops.
One he opened as a butcher's,
Where he sold steaks and joints and chops.

A mate of his was keen on birds,
And opened up The Aviary.
A venture which, if honest,
Farmer Avery found *unsavioury*.

Another mate liked bees,
So he opened up The Apiery.
A vintner sold off excess fruit,
And called his shop the Grapery.
A Frenchman had a snackbar,
Which, of course, he called Le Creperie.

An ex-soldier sold medals,
And his shop was just called Bravery.
A cook sold sausage rolls and pies,
In a shop he named The Savoury,
Not to be confused with a missionary,
Who opened up The Savery.

Behind the Rhymes

Another chef brewed sauces,
His shop he called The Gravery.
Another sold pre-packaged snacks,
From what he called The Quavery.

Someone opened up a stationer,
Which he grandly called The Papery.
As vaping was the latest trend,
Someone opened up The Vapery.

And a builder who laid pavements,
Opened up The Pavery.
A young entrepreneur,
Ran a nightclub called The Ravery.

There was a joke shop called The Japery,
And another called The Capery.
But Farmer Avery drew the line,
At selling monkeys in an apery.

Farmer Avery put a flier round,
After hours of contemplation.
It was designed to lead the local folk
Into retail temptation.

It said…

Behind the Rhymes

"Shop at Farmer Avery's for The Aviary, The Apiary, The Grapery, Le Creperie, Bravery, The Savoury, The Savery, The Gravery, The Quavery, The Papery, The Japery, The Vapery, The Capery, The Pavery, The Ravery... and:
... a butcher's."

101

Behind the Rhymes

WANDERING WONDERING WHY

One Wednesday we were walking,
In West Somerset countryside,
The weather was wet and windy,
With vistas wild and wide.

Thoughts veered off on a tangent,
As I marvelled at the view,
Why do so many local villages,
Began with double-U?

Places beginning X and Z,
There are absolutely none.
And is Yarde the solitary Y?
 V? … Vellow is the only one.

And Upton also stands alone,
In starting with a U,
There's no F, no G, no J,
And, understandably, no Q.

Yet there's Withypool and Williton,
West Quantoxhead and Winsford,
Watchet, Weacombe, Wootton Courtney,
Wheddon Cross and Woodford.
There's a gardeners' shop at Wibble,
There's Watersmeet and Wiveliscombe,
And a hamlet, Withiel Florey,
Then there's Washford and there's Withycombe.

This problem's kept me up at night,
Wondering why the letter's prevalent,
But then I thought, "Why worry?
It weally is not welevant."

DRINKERS

I've seen thin people drink coffee.
I've seen skinny girls drink tea,
And slim men drinking water,
Is familiar to me.

I've seen svelte maids sipping fruit juice,
And slender chaps drink beer,
And lean people with water,
Is quite common around here.

I've watched slight ladies with vodka,
And boney men with gin,
And waif-like girls with orange squash,
And wine drinkers who are thin.

But I find it quite ironic,
When I'm watching folk,
That I only see fat people,
Drinking Diet Coke.

UNDERSTANDING LSD

So darling, you would like to know,
How money used to be,
I'll explain as simply as I can,
Come, sit upon my knee.

There were twenty shillings in one pound,
And twelve pence made a shilling,
And so two hundred and forty pence,
Made a pound, is that not thrilling?

A pound was often called a quid,
It could also be a knicker,
with both, the plural's never used,
Which made their use much slicker.

Another name using singular,
Was bob, a name for shilling
Five bob could also be a dollar,
I'll go on dear, if you're willing.

Half a penny was a ha'penny,
Two pence were known as tuppence,
And when they weren't called threppence,
Three pence were known as thruppence.

Behind the Rhymes

A farthing was a penny,
Divided into four,
Or a ha'penny split in two,
Please listen dear, there's more.

Pennies, ha'pennies and farthings,
Were lumped together as coppers,
That's right dear, as were policemen,
No dear, it did not confuse the shoppers.

Now, sixpence was a tanner,
Five shillings was a crown,
And half a crown was two and six,
Now dear, please sit down.

Please listen dear, I'm nearly done,
Two shillings was a florin,
Two and six was half a dollar.
No dear it's not foreign.

One pound one shilling made a guinea,
No dear, I don't know why,
OK, OK, we'll leave it there,
And darling please don't cry.

Behind the Rhymes

THE END

Behind the Rhymes

Printed in Poland
by Amazon Fulfillment
Poland Sp. z o.o., Wrocław